Grayslake Area Public Library District
Grayslake, Illinois

1. A fine will be charged on each book which is not returned when it is due.

2. All injuries to books beyond reasonable wear and all losses shall be made good to the satisfaction of the Librarian.

3. Each borrower is held responsible for all books drawn on his card and for all fines accruing on the same.

DEMCO

The Tortoise and the Hare

Simon & Schuster Books for Young Readers
An imprint of Simon & Schuster Children's Publishing Division
1230 Avenue of the Americas
New York, NY 10020

The text for this book was set in Utopia.
Printed and bound in the United States of America
10 9 8 7 6 5 4 3

The Library of Congress has cataloged the Simon & Schuster
Books for Young Readers Edition as follows:
Miles, Betty.
The tortoise and the hare / by Betty Miles ; illustrated by Paul Meisel.
p. cm. — (Ready-to-read)
Summary: Recounts in simple dialogue the famous tale of the
race between the persevering turtle and the boastful rabbit.
ISBN 0-689-81792-4
[1. Fables. 2. Folklore.] I. Aesop. II. Meisel, Paul, ill.
III. Hare and the tortoise. IV. Title. V. Series.
PZ8.2.M485To 1998
398.2—dc21 [E] 97-17355
CIP   AC

The Tortoise and the Hare

By Betty Miles
Illustrated by Paul Meisel

Ready-to-Read

Simon & Schuster Books for Young Readers

OLD STORIES FOR NEW READERS

The Tortoise and the Hare is an old story, and old stories are good for new readers. When they know what is going to happen, it's easier to read the words that tell about it.

Old stories often use the same words, like "One step, another step" over and over again. A new reader begins to expect those words, to enjoy them, and to learn them. Even a hard word like "Tortoise" becomes easy when you see it many times.

You give your new reader a good start when you read out loud to each other. In this book, all the words are the animals' talk. Your child can read one animal's words and you can read another's.

Take time to enjoy the story and the pictures. You can help your reader by talking about what is happening on the page and what might happen next. You can point to familiar words in the pictures. You can point to words that rhyme, and you can help by asking what sound a word begins with.

Most of all, you can help by reading together often. Your new reader can read with you or with a grandparent, a babysitter, an older brother, sister, or a friend. New readers love to share their books!

Hey! Look at me!
Look at me run!

I can run faster than you, Squirrel.
Faster than you, Fox.

Faster than you, Bear.
Faster than you, Mouse.
6   I can run faster than anyone!

Faster than me?

Ha, ha, Tortoise!
Of course I can run
faster than you!
I can run faster
than anyone.
And you are slower
than anyone!

Oh, yes?
Do you want to race?

9

Race with you?
Ha, ha, ha!
Of course I will
race with you—
and I will win!

We will see.
I am slow,
but I am steady.
We will see
who wins.

A race! A race!

Let me be
the referee!
OK, Tortoise?
OK, Hare?

OK. Thank you,
Mouse.

OK. Let's go!

You will run
around the lake.

Ha ha, Tortoise!
I can run
around the lake
faster than you.

We will see!

13

OK, Tortoise
and Hare.
Get ready,
get set,
GO!

Go, Hare!
Go, Tortoise!

One step and
another step.
I am slow,
but I am steady.

I am fast, fast, fast!
Look at me run!

One step, another step.
One step and another.
Slow and steady.

Tortoise is so slow
I can take a little rest.
Zzzzzzzzzzzzzzz.

One step
and another
and another.

ZZZZZZZZZZZZZ.

Can you see Hare?
Can you see Tortoise?

22

No!

23

Zzzzzzzzzzz.

One step, another step.
One step and another.

25

Slow and steady.

One step and another.
I can do it!

Look!

Tortoise!

28

One step,
another step.

Oh! The race!

Tortoise!
TORTOISE!

Tortoise wins!
YAY, TORTOISE!

31

I am slow,
but I am steady.
And I am the winner!

THE END